AF269143

TALES

FROM AN ODD MIND

NOM D. PLUME

TALES FROM AN ODD MIND
Copyright © Nom D. Plume Enterprises, 2020
All rights reserved.

PUBLISHER'S NOTE:
These are works of fiction. Names, characters, places, businesses, and incidents are either the product of the author's imagination or are used fictitiously, and any resemblance to actual persons, living or dead, or to places, businesses, or incidents, is entirely coincidental.

https://www.talesfromanoddmind.com

ISBN 978-1-7348864-0-5 (paperback)
ISBN 978-1-7348864-2-9 (ebook)

For everyone who helped and inspired me on this odd and
wonderful journey. There are too many of you to name, but I
carry you all in my heart and in my mind always.

My special appreciation of course, to the authors of the past who
provide me with works to read and ideas to challenge.

INTRODUCTION:

Some words from Death

FIRST SECTION:

CHAPTER ONES

The beginnings of several tales whose endings have yet to be told

SECOND SECTION:

WE FEW OLD SOULS

A quintet of tales of several young people who find each other, time after time

THIRD SECTION:

POETRY AND PROSE

No rhymes, some reason

INTRODUCTION

Hello there, dear reader.

My name is Death.

A bit morbid, I know, to have me introducing this book. A bit morbid to even think of me, really. But our author has a very odd mind and has decided for some very odd reason to invoke a muse.

So, here I am.

I realize that it is quite the irony to have me beginning something, but I've never quite had the opportunity to before, so I suppose this will be an adventure for both of us.

But since the author has promised me this whole page to talk, I suppose I will use just a bit more of this space.

When I gaze upon those who have passed on, I see their lives as one would peer into a foggy glass. Not a full picture of what lies inside, but just enough to get a sense of that person, in the never-ending sea of life.

Much like the stories you will read after this, a look into pieces of distant worlds, or lives right next door. Of people who have lived and will die, but who will never be forgotten.

Well, then.

Shall we begin?

CHAPTER ONE

CHAPTER ONE

Off the Map

DARREN HAD TO RUN to catch up with Samuel. Samuel had said that there was a rare species of *Mortem flos* up ahead and he absolutely needed to document it. And then Samuel had used his ridiculously long legs to dash up the path and Darren was stuck running after him.

Darren came panting up behind Samuel a few minutes later, cursing his asthma the entire time.

Samuel had bent down and was no longer a full two feet taller than Darren. He held up a hand for Darren to stop, and pointed to the flower he was sketching. It was as black as the night and had a bright red stem. Samuel had the sketch almost finished in one of his huge leather-bound books.

Samuel had said that he was going to document every plant, every animal, every species that existed in the world. Darren had thought it pointless at first, an idiot on an idiotic quest, but discovered that Samuel had three huge bound books just from the deserts to the south.

And those were completed before Darren had ever met him. After they had met, Samuel had said that they were going to this forest, and Darren had no room to argue.

Samuel seemed very much at home in this forest, which was not on any map that any reasonable person had.

Darren thought that Samuel seemed to see him as a young tree, something that could be guided and molded, and Samuel had been training him in their short time together. And Samuel loved his flowers.

"Cut it off just before the root, Darren," Samuel murmured, as if the flower could hear them.

Darren took a pair of clippers out of his bag and did as Samuel asked. He had been learning how to do what was more or less gardening and note keeping. He was good enough at the former for Samuel to let him gather flower samples.

Samuel carefully put the cut flower in a small bag in his backpack. His bag was enchanted, and would keep the flowers fresh, and he kept the bag organized to a T.

Samuel scratched his long reddish beard and said, "Come, there is more to see."

Darren sighed. "Can't we just rest? I'm tired, Samuel."

Darren sat down on a rock.

Samuel shook his head.

"You should not camp near a *Mortem flos,* Darren, strange things happen to those who do. Come." He clapped his hands. "I shall carry you until we can reach a campsite."

Darren was too surprised to protest when Samuel shifted his large backpack to one shoulder and put him on his back.

Darren looked over the top of Samuel's odd woven hat and wiped his glasses a few times to make sure he saw everything clearly. The view was certainly different from almost seven feet up than it was at about five. He could see the tallest branches instead of tripping over overgrown roots.

Samuel marched through the forest for what seemed like hours, chasing the sun until they reached a place free of trees.

Then Samuel put Darren down and Darren looked over the cliff they were on, over the never-ending forest and fiery sky of the setting sun.

He couldn't bring himself to look back. He promised himself that he would never look back.

Samuel made Darren help with parts of the campsite. Darren tried and failed to set up a tent and Samuel showed him how to make some stew that smelled foul but tasted like rosemary.

Darren wrapped the blankets around himself many times and sat in the tent shivering, until Samuel said to come out. It was even colder out there.

Samuel spent the rest of the night teaching Darren about the constellations and Darren tried very hard to remember what Samuel said about their stories and powers, but it was very late and very cold.

*   *   *

Darren woke up covered in blankets and Samuel's jacket. Samuel was talking and laughing in his booming voice to some woodland spirits that had come to visit.

Each sprite was only as big as a fist. They were pure green, although there were varying shades. The little balls squeaked in delight right along with Samuel's laughter.

"Oh Darren!" Samuel said. "Come here, I should teach you to talk with them!"

Darren rubbed his eyes and glasses and walked over and sat by Samuel.

Samuel explained that the chattering and squeaking meant different things–Samuel had already written down their language in one of his books.

They talked and Darren did his best to answer until lunch.

The sun was high in the sky and the sky was free of clouds. Darren did his best to pack up the supplies and Samuel helped him with most of it.

They walked along for most of the day in silence, as Samuel always said to listen to the trees and Darren had no idea what that meant but he tried.

Later, Samuel walked ahead, as he often did, and started to sing a wordless melody that felt a thousand years old.

"Hello."

Darren stopped short.

In front of him stood a girl about his age who had a black cloak on. She had hair as red as fresh blood and she seemed to blend in with the trees.

Darren let out a shaky "H-Hello."

Samuel had stopped and said, "Darren? Where are you?"

"Oh, down here I just met—"

"Fleur," the girl said. "My name is Fleur."

"Well hello Fleur," Samuel said in his booming voice, looking back to meet them. "Will you be coming with us?"

Fleur looked at him and smiled, "I believe I will."

"Where are your feet?" Darren asked.

He had only now noticed that her feet were—-well, nowhere; she seemed to float, never quite touching the ground, where her feet would be was just air.

Samuel and Fleur looked at him like he was an idiot.

"She's a ghost."

"Oh."

Fleur kept watch over the camp that night, and she and Samuel stayed up all night talking about the stars.

Fleur also stayed back with Darren and talked with him when Samuel went plowing on ahead.

She helped Samuel with the ghost part of his journals, and Samuel was very thankful for the help.

"Are you going to stay with us then?" Darren asked one night, when Fleur was sitting on a rock staring at the moon.

"Well," Fleur smiled, "I suppose I'm following Samuel for the same reason you are."

"And that is?" Darren asked.

Fleur had a sad smile on her face when she turned her eyes back to the bright blue moon and said:

"I don't have anywhere else to go."

Both of them were silent for a while and then Fleur said, "Where are we going?"

Darren looked up into the sky of endless stars and looked at a constellation Samuel had shown him.

"North," said Darren. "We're going north."

WOLF

&

RAVEN

WOLF AND RAVEN SAT on a stone bench at the end of the pier looking over the inky black water.

It was almost three in the morning and the sleepy little fishing town was all asleep. Not a single lantern was lit. The few police awake often didn't patrol to the edge of the pier, which was convenient since Wolf and Raven looked incredibly suspicious.

Raven's suit was a mess; the button holding the jacket together had been torn off and the jacket was spattered with drying blood. Wolf had set her nose but it was going to be crooked for a while.

Wolf didn't look much better. His jeans were covered in just as much blood as Raven's suit and his curly hair had several clumps missing.

The brown paper bag that held the things they had bought at the local market was sitting between them, already having been emptied for the bandages and iodine.

Wolf pulled the bag closer to himself and rummaged around until he found the Whirly Pop they had bought. He yanked the plastic wrapping off and contemplated the rainbow colors before the dark night.

"That went well." He brought the pop to his mouth.

"That did not even *remotely* go well," Raven mumbled. She foraged around inside the bag until she found the Milky Way and took off the wrapper. "Did you have to take the Whirly Pop?"

"Yes. And it could have gone considerably worse."

"Well that's because almost *anything* can go more wrong than it already has."

"Did you get hit on the head? That didn't make much sense."

"You know damn well I got knocked on the head—"

"Which is why I wanted to get you frozen peas but nooo—"

"They would have soaked through the bag and ruined the gauze and the bandages."

"Well do you want to go back into the town and get frozen peas now?"

"We look like we just stabbed fifty men to death, they'll call the police."

"They didn't call the first time we went into the store."

"The guy behind the register was clearly high, he'll think it was some bad trip—"

"So, let's go back, it's open 24 hours—"

"It'll be way past that guy's shift and I don't want to give anyone in town a second look at us."

"Fine. How much longer till pickup?"

"They said they'd be here forty-five minutes ago."

"They would just leave us here, wouldn't they?"

"They would."

"We could just listen to music while we wait. My phone wasn't damaged."

"True."

Wolf pulled out his phone and set his music to shuffle.

"I hate this song."

"You just have no appreciation for good music."

"I know good music. This isn't it."

"*Why* are we partners?"

"Because I said yes. And because you have no idea how to talk to people."

"You have no idea how planning works."

"I do actually, but fine. For the sake of argument, you're here for planning, and I'm here to make sure we don't get fired."

"*I* make sure we don't get fired."

"Sure you do."

"They're almost an hour late. We're probably going to have to take the bus back."

"I saw a bus station and a popsicle stand next to the fishmongers."

"That could work. Just like Venice."

"We're still not speaking about Venice."

"Fine. But they're not here."

"Yeah…but if they're making us wait, we should make them wait."

"I think the donut shop opens in ten minutes."

"We still look like axe murderers."

"Just take your jacket off, I'll turn my jeans inside out—"

"That's not going to help."

"They're black jeans, it won't be noticeable."

"Should we charge the fee to the agency?"

"Hell yes."

"Sounds like a plan."

"After you then."

BOX

OF

J.O.Y.

THERE WERE ALTOGETHER MANY things that could've been in the box Leonard found after the fight club. There could have been drugs, or money, or body parts. (Dr. Manchester would've *loved* it if there were body parts, they were much harder to find when one was trying to keep on the straight and narrow.) Those would at least be expected in that part of the city. But there was nothing like that when Leonard pried open the front of the box with the long knife that Griffith was *definitely* not supposed to bring to the club. Griffith didn't care though, and there wasn't a being in the universe that could take his blades away from him.

"What…is that?" Leonard said when the front creaked open.

Griffith gave him a shit-eating grin. The same grin that Leonard had gotten so many times before, usually when he was the only one left out of a plan until the last minute.

"That, my friend, is what you call a child."

Leonard scowled at him, and since he still hadn't wiped the blood off his face, it was quite intimidating.

Griffith didn't care.

Dr. Manchester looked down at the small child in the crate and said, "What is your name, little one?"

Dr. Manchester even knelt to look less threatening, not that it helped much.

What was terrifying about him wasn't an odd tallness, like Leonard; or eyes that were so dark, one was frightened by looking into them, like Griffith.

It was his smile.

Dr. Manchester really only had two smiles, a very soft and kind one that only Leonard and Griffith had been privy to, and a face-splitting grin that he usually had on for surgeries. Or dissections. Or fights. And for some reason that was the smile that he gave to the child. The child looked up at him though, blankly, and utterly unterrified. Then they blinked and held up two small metal disks.

"Why would a child have dog tags, I wonder?" Griffith said while Dr. Manchester inspected them.

"Griffith, you speak French, correct?" Dr. Manchester asked.

It was a question they all knew the answer to. Griffith spoke more languages than even he could keep track of, but Dr. Manchester tended to rattle on when he was nervous.

Neither of the other men mentioned it.

"*Oui*," Griffith said, and when Dr. Manchester tossed the tags over he inspected them with Leonard reading over his shoulder. Leonard had assumed his natural position when he didn't like a situation, utterly silent and so still people had thought he was a scarecrow at one point.

"Hmmm," Griffith said, "the child doesn't have a name but they are from Project J.O.Y."

A sudden chill came over the three men even though it was a sticky July night.

Not that any of them would admit it.

They could have left the child there in that box on the street outside the fight club and gone home with their consciences clean—they had all run into J.O.Y. in their previous professions and weren't eager to do so again. It wouldn't even have been the worst thing they'd done.

Not even in the top ten.

They didn't. And they all wondered why they hadn't for years after the fact.

They never came up with a satisfactory answer.

*   *   *

The child was fast asleep when Leonard carried them through the door. They had locked eyes with Leonard and hadn't let anyone else carry them. Leonard was actually the best one with children but hated to be near them.

The small apartment was all the three men could afford when their last job had shut down. Griffith had haggled over the price with the landlord for three hours and they had only been allowed to move in when Leonard started discussing, in detail, all the ways he knew to dispose of a body. The landlord had left them alone after that, but they always found a way to pay their rent and as long as no police were called, no one had any problems.

Well, they didn't have any problems with the landlord.

They all had more issues than any of them would ever admit.

They set the child down on the worn couch and Dr. Manchester gave them a quick checkup.

He pronounced the child was healthy with only a few bandages needed. "Only a few bandages needed" was more or less "glowing with health" as far as they were concerned.

Since there was only one bedroom with one bed, and since they decided the child would have it that night (for the sake of privacy and quiet), the men agreed to sleep at various places in the living room and the kitchen.

Leonard sprawled on the floor, Dr. Manchester took the couch (claiming his back problems), and Griffith said that he would take the tile floor in the kitchen.

None of them slept much that night, but they never really did, kept awake by nightmares, memories, or old paranoias making themselves known.

Griffith was smoking one of his emergency cigarettes when Leonard nudged him. "Dr. Manchester will kill you if he catches you smoking. 'Specially around the kid."

Griffith let out a long plume of smoke and smiled. "That is why I am very good at not being caught."

He nodded his head to the already-open window. The smell would be gone by morning. Leonard groaned and dragged a hand over his face, then stared out of the small window onto the crumbling city.

Neither of them mentioned the times he had been caught.

"Cas always wanted kids y'know?"

The only reason Griffith didn't even raise an eyebrow at that was years of training his face to fit whatever mask was needed at that moment. Cas was strictly off limits for discussion unless Leonard brought her up, and he almost never did.

Not even today.

So Griffith just nodded.

Leonard had really only fallen in love once, and it was to Cas, a snarky assassin quite like him. Cas had been nice enough but was deadly on the battlefield. That was the reason Griffith had always liked her.

Dr. Manchester always liked her because she would smuggle him Scotch.

Cas and Leonard had been together for five years, which was longer than any relationship anyone in their old job could have hoped for. Then one day she just wasn't fast enough and Leonard hadn't come out of his room for weeks. He almost never talked about her except for today—which was her birthday and her death day.

Which is why they had all gone to the club to let off some steam.

Leonard didn't say anything more and Griffith didn't push it. Leonard hardly ever said anything about Cas at all, even though he still wore her lucky red bandana around his arm.

"We are going to keep the child then?" Griffith asked.

It wasn't really his decision to make, or Leonard's, or even Dr. Manchester's. From the second the child had put their arms up for Leonard they all knew they would keep the child

Leonard shrugged like he hadn't come to the same conclusion. "Yeah…"

He looked out the window, like the polluted sky had the answers for the questions he wouldn't ask.

Griffith almost wanted to ask if Leonard wanted to name the child Cas, but decided not to.

Enough of the past had been dragged up already.

A BLACK DOG,

A GRAVEYARD,

AND THE SEA

THE FIRST THING I can think is more of a scream, muffled and terrified.

I can't breathe, I can't see!

I realize with a start that it's because there is dirt everywhere, covering me completely and blocking off my air.

There is a faint scratching above me, insistent and relentless. I don't think I was buried in a coffin and I don't know if I want to know what's coming for me.

I don't know if I want it to find me.

But then it does and my eyes are blinded by the moonlight.

I cough and realize that I'm lying in what used to be my grave with a huge black dog sitting on its haunches looking at me like I'm his favorite person in the world.

The graveyard is filled with different types of stones. Simple ones grown over with moss, marble ones in a straight row, and a few mausoleums that cast shadows almost as big as the trees that surround the place.

The dog moves forward and nuzzles me with his face. I'm able to see his collar then and it has a tag on it. It looks ancient and there is only one word carved onto it: FIRST.

"First?" I say. My throat sounds a wreck from the dirt and underuse…how long have I been dead?

First pants happily and flops down on my lap, "I know you, don't I?" First looks at me with eyes that are too red for my tastes and whines. "Of course, you couldn't tell me even if you knew."

I'm able to turn my torso just enough to look at my headstone. I've been dead for a while.

Under my name…

Grey Jones 1844-1865

…is a more recent addition:

The Devil's son

buried in his finery

and with his loved one

"Loved one…" I turn around as much as I can to look at what used to be my grave but there's no one else there, "First?" His ears perk up. "Who is my loved one?"

First gets up and starts to dig behind me.

After a minute his teeth clamp against something and he comes back and drops whatever it is in my lap and sits back down looking very proud of himself.

It's about three feet long and is covered in dirt except for where First's teeth have been, where a rusted metal is starting to peek through.

I look down at my lap properly this time and see that I am indeed in all my finery. I'm in a very well-cut suit that has held up remarkably well considering I've been dead for almost 200 years.

I uncover whatever is in my lap to find a sword. Not a decorative military sword, not a fencing sword, a light one-and-half sword. Perfect for fighting. It fits my grip and reflects the moonlight perfectly.

"This is what I loved?"

First just snorts and lies back on my lap. I rub the back of his head and start to think.

I'm alive now. But why?

That's when the moon decides to tell me, or at least show me.

For a split second I'm on a beach, the sand is white and there are plants sticking up through the sand for just a few inches. There's a lighthouse in the distance and three people waiting for me.

They could be waiting for anyone of course; they're just standing there and watching but somehow, I just *know* they're waiting for me.

Then the sea starts to moan and the sky darkens. Something is coming, I don't know what but it's ancient and it's dangerous.

Find us

The people are still unmoving but their voices carry loud and clear

Find us!

In a second, I'm back in the graveyard with First licking my hand. It had already found its way to the blade while I was in the trance.

"Hey boy," I mumble, putting the sword down and scratching behind his ears.

For some reason I know where the lighthouse is. I never saw the lighthouse before in my life, and I didn't see the address on it but it's in Massachusetts. I could find it exactly if I was in the town next to it, even hidden in a bay as it is.

Now if only I knew where *I* was.

First sits up suddenly and I get the feeling that he's telling me it's time to go. So, I stand, put the sword in my belt and walk out of the graveyard with First by my side.

The moon will guide me, I don't know how I know but I know.

I just know.

A Warped View of the Stars

GUARDSMAN X37 WATCHED THE stars from his makeshift prison in the engine room with a sour taste in his mouth and a sinking feeling. Every star that slipped by was one farther than he wanted to go.

He wanted to punch the rough metal wall and curse his luck. His luck had never been the best but this seemed just downright cruel. He had been captured by outlaws by complete accident. Not as a hostage for an important prisoner transfer, or even a souvenir. By *accident.*

His hands were tied over his head and he had no idea how to get past the huge man who was sitting across from him; who watched his every move and had his finger firmly on his plasma rifle's trigger. Guardsman X37 had attempted a smile at first, just for formalities' sake but the scowl from the man sent all thoughts of formalities from his head.

The man had been incredibly angry when he hadn't been able to kill Guardsman X37, and the captain, the legendary outlaw Cynthia

Rose, had intervened and said, "We aren't killing him, Oswald. He's barely a child."

"He's old enough! His people kill children! They tried to kill everyone on this ship and in our fleet."

"Which is why we aren't going to kill him, Oswald. Understood?"

And that had been the end of that. Oswald had shut his mouth and tied up Guardsman X37 in the engine room. Guardsman X37 hadn't been quite awake enough to contribute to the conversation but he had been very awake when the heavy door to the engine room slammed shut and the engineer had actually jumped.

The engineer, Kit, seemed to be a bit chattier, as chatty as she could be since everyone on the crew seemed ready to drop dead of exhaustion. The battle hadn't been easy on anyone. She had introduced herself quickly and then went back to the engine. She mumbled to herself as she tinkered, with her small circular robots overhead to help her.

The robots broke at least four regulations. Guardsman X37 usually never cared much for regulation unless they were egregious violations but running them through his head was the only thing that seemed to calm him. The battle at the last planet had been long and grueling. The outlaws had barely succeeded in stealing the heir and the heir's servants. Again. It had been unexpected the first time, annoying the second, and downright humiliating the third time. The band of outlaws had in fact stolen every heir of the Zodiac system; Guardsman X37's unit had been sent in to try to prevent the final capture and they had failed. Just like every other time any special forces had tried to stop them.

They had figured out far too late that it wasn't inside information or new technology that was enabling the outlaws to make attack after successful attack, it was Cynthia Rose. And Cynthis Rose was incredibly dangerous. There were even rumors she had joined…

Guardsman X37's eyes caught a purple flag with a black raven on it that hung above Kit's hammock.

The rumors were true then. The ship and Cynthia Rose were part of the terrorist organization The Seventh Band. Guardsman X37 groaned silently. The terrorists in The Seventh Band were the bane of the Government's existence. Guardsman X37's major had railed about them almost every day to the point that Guardsman X37's friend Enzo could do a spot-on impression.

Guardsman X37 tried not to think of Enzo, or Blue, Cea, Wolf, or any of his old friends. He didn't think of Enzo's smile, or of how Blue could recite poetry from memory. He definitely didn't think of how Cea could walk off the battlefield and still drink them all under the table. He refused to think of Wolf's protectiveness that had helped him get into the Guardsman unit in the first place.

He had to focus.

The Seventh Band were killers. They had killed generals and soldiers alike; they had freed heinous criminals in raids and had blown up communication and transportation hubs. And Guardsman X37 was their prisoner. He estimated about a 30% survival rate but without a calculator it was hard to be sure.

They had taken his plasma rifle, his handgun, and his knives. If he escaped, he would have to use his fists to fight before he could get a weapon. The manacles that held his wrists were incredibly strong; he had tested them. Even if he dislocated his thumbs, he couldn't slip them off, and there was no keyhole, so Guardsman X37 was faced with the unfortunate conclusion that they were dwarf star shackles. Which was more concerning because that meant there had to be a Raik on board who could manipulate the complicated and dense material that was dwarf star metal. Which was another problem. How do you kill someone who can manipulate the very atoms of the weapon you're fighting them with?

A problem for another time.

Maybe though…just maybe the Raik was a child. There were rumors that the twin heirs of Gemini, Winter and Summer, were Raiks, and they were only eight years old. Oswald had covered Guardsman X37's eyes when his cuffs had been sealed, so maybe the children had done it.

Maybe they would undo it. But that was unlikely without a threat of force, which he couldn't muster without getting out of the shackles in the first place.

Maybe he could get Oswald to unlock them for him. No, the man hated him. Maybe Kit…but she seemed so focused that even if Oswald wasn't watching his every move he couldn't signal to her. And there would be no reason for her to free him.

Then there was the question of what he was going to do if he did get free. Leave, obviously; but he had no idea how long he had been asleep and had no idea where they were.

Guardsman X37 didn't have much time to think on that because there were the tell-tale sounds of combat boots coming down the metal stairs and both Kit and Oswald stood up to salute their captain, Cynthia Rose.

Cynthia Rose was just as intimidating as the wanted posters said she would be. She was six feet tall with arms that could—and would—snap necks. She wore the purple emblem of The Seventh Band on her jacket sleeve. Guardsman X37 told himself that he wasn't afraid, but he'd always been a terrible liar.

Oswald nodded sharply. "Captain."

"Oswald. Kit. If you don't mind, I'd like a word alone with our prisoner."

The two shared a look, and Oswald said, "Captain, at least carry a weapon. He's dangerous."

"Oswald, there's nowhere he can go. I'll be fine. Thank you for your concern."

The two went up the stairs and Oswald shot Guardsman X37 a withering look. Guardsman X37 was temped to stick his tongue out in response but that would have been unprofessional. Getting captured was also unprofessional but he didn't have much time to think it over before the outlaw began to speak.

"Well then." Cynthia Rose smiled, sitting on the floor in front of Guardsman X37. "Welcome to my humble ship. I suppose we have a lot to talk about, don't we?"

"We don't. You will release me at the next port and hand yourself over to the authorities." Guardsman X37 was sure his voice did not sound nearly as strong as it needed to.

She smirked. "Oh will I?"

He locked eyes with her, "Yes."

"I'm afraid that's not possible. First off, we're almost past the last port now, second, we're being chased by so many of your people that we simply cannot slow down. Thirdly, I don't give a fuck what any follower of that puppet government says."

Well, that settled that possibility. "Where are we going then?"

"Why should I tell you?"

"You wanted this meeting, therefore you have something to tell me. You wouldn't call your people out of the room just to taunt me."

"True, I'm here to tell you of your situation. Do you know what ship you are on?"

"The Silver Wolf: wanted for theft in three separate systems, 34 smuggling counts, part of The Seventh Band's fleet—"

"Aww, are you trying to make me blush?"

Guardsman X37 just scowled.

She waved a hand. "Anyway, yes, you are on the Silver Wolf and you are our prisoner. We and the rest of our fleet are currently heading towards the belt of lost planets."

"Why are you telling me this?"

"Because even if you could get out of those shackles, and you can't, manage to kill everyone on this ship—which is hilariously impossible—and somehow take over the ship and transmit our coordinates and plans to your superiors, we'd be long gone when they show up and you would be blasted from the sky by the fleet."

"I know that. But you came down here to tell me something, and it wasn't that I can't escape."

Cynthia Rose's smirk softened at that. "True, we—the heirs and the crew—want to give you what amounts to your last words."

Guardsman X37 shoved down the dread that washed over him, but he supposed that death, even a slow one, would be better than being their prisoner. "So, you are going to kill me. Even after that whole speech to Oswald."

Cynthia Rose was about thirty, but in that moment she looked very ancient, and very tired. "What I said still stands. We won't kill you but I think you've realized on some level that you can never go back."

Guardsman X37 knew. The belt of lost planets was on the very edge of the galaxy, past asteroid fields littered with bombs, past every hint of civilization; it was the galaxy's garbage dump. Planets that couldn't be terraformed to fit any life form, rogue planets that were disturbing systems, and resource planets that had been used up, that were just useless husks.

Guardsman X37 had no idea how to fly a ship, much less navigate one through all the pitfalls between the lost planets and the galaxy, and The Seventh Band would never let him go. Ironically of course, if he were just in the infantry instead of being a Guardsman the security might have been laxer and he could have been able to escape.

But he was a Guardsman. And a Guardsman to The Seventh Band was something of a boogeyman. Not that that was his fault, the Guardsman had made their reputation hundreds of years before he became one.

He was a boogeyman that could never go home. Could never again see his friends or his home planet. How in the world would they react when he was declared dead or missing in action?

Guardsman X37 hoped he would be declared dead; "missing in action" would only give them false hope.

"I know."

"So, you can record a short message and we'll send it out to the ships that are chasing us. They won't slow down or even stop, but I'd feel bad if your family never knew what happened to you."

She said it like she expected Guardsman X37 to say "I don't have or need a family" or something to that effect. His friends were his family without a doubt, but he did have a family, with two younger siblings who went to school on the wages he earned from being a Guardsman. What would happen to them?

"Thank you. I know they would stay up all night otherwise."

She scowled but said, "You have siblings?"

"Two. Younger. And my friends in my unit are just about my siblings too."

"I had an older one for a few years," she said. "Then he got himself caught in a transport mechanism when he was drunk out of his mind."

They both sat there for a second, the odd moment of kindness sitting there before it flitted away.

"You have two minutes to think of your message." She stood and went to the stairs then paused. "I wonder if they'll hail you as a martyr or condemn you as a traitor."

It only took him a minute and thirty seconds. Cynthia Rose came back exactly two minutes later with a recorder.

Guardsman X37 took a deep breath and started his speech.

"This is Guardsman X37 of Unit 19 under command of Major Seth. I have been captured by The Seventh Band and there is no feasible option for escape. I want to make clear that I have not joined the terrorists and will not do so."

He paused; that was all he needed to say, legally. His sisters and family would receive financial aid and his unit and friends would be untouched. He added:

"Bella, Celeste, I'm sorry I couldn't be there for your next birthdays but I promise I'll still celebrate them. Wolf, Cea, Enzo, Blue, thank you so much for being my friends, I'll never forget you. Mom, Dad, I'll try to be home soon."

Cynthia Rose turned off the recorder and went up the stairs without another word, and Guardsman X37 was again left alone with the stars.

PROJECT KAGE

THE HEAVY METAL DOORS that are supposed to guard the control room from whatever probably illegal experiments were in the basement are torn from their hinges and imbedded in the opposite wall. Something must have escaped. Something powerful. Not that Command gave any other orders besides "Investigate the station to see what has been wreaking havoc in our navigating satellites."

We had a fun time getting here since we had to fly by sight with a blizzard coming in but we made it okay. I don't think whoever was in here was so lucky.

We've split up to investigate everything that has already gone wrong and I bravely volunteered to take the only place with the heat still on. Collin turned the rest of the power back on a few minutes ago.

Whatever escaped didn't destroy the control grid, just shorted it out. But it must have been brutally powerful; there are cracks in the thick windows.

Still, nothing got through.

Whatever escaped from Arctic Station #17 five long years ago is still here with us. Somewhere. I just need to find it. Preferably before my team does.

Daniel calls in. "Captain Reed? I found the lab. You need to get down here now."

"Copy that," I answer. "On my way."

I am in charge of Special Forces Squad Raptor 12. My team was sent to this base to investigate the disappearance five years ago of the ten soldiers and three scientists who were stationed here.

We are now here to find out what happened and if possible, bring in whatever did it. This is a completely covert mission, no backup. If we drop off comms, they declare us dead.

We've made great progress so far.

We have determined that all thirteen ran outside the base before freezing to death; we found their bodies before we even got in. We have determined that whatever the scientists were working on got out and wreaked havoc on the base.

The files say it was "Project Kage" and was years in the making. But when all the comms went dead five years ago, Command apparently didn't care about their very important project and only called us in because weird signals have been traced back here.

If we find whatever did this, we can secure it and bring it back and we can all probably get a week's rest, and maybe even some promotions. I think Colonel Ava Reed would sound very nice, myself.

There's just one problem: Command thinks we're dead.

The comm went out a few minutes after we entered the station, like there was a dampening field just around us. At least that's what I told the rest of the team.

Even though the station is still perfectly sealed from the outside, it feels like the Arctic is slowly seeping in.

I go down to see Daniel in the lab. If it can even be called a lab anymore. When I arrive, it's in the same state as the control room, in complete shambles, but there's a shadowy vapor swirling around in it.

"I found more of the file, Captain," Blake says, coming up from the archives. "Whatever this is used to be human."

"Did it now?" I ask, moving further into the lab. The shadows close in, become thicker. The cold becomes almost crushing.

"This is… incredibly illegal," Blake mumbles, still looking at the file. "They took the kid when they couldn't be more than ten or eleven, lied to their family. We need to call command they need to know about this—"

"Comms are down, Blake," I say, maybe too calmly. I'm almost in the middle of the room now. Command already knows. They've always known.

The shadows suddenly swoop down on me as Blake yells, "Captain, watch out!"

But nothing happens. The shadows swirl around me, examining me, looking with a million eyes and finally seem placated. The shadows form in front of me and I hear the group's guns cocking behind me.

"Hold your fire!" I yell. The shadows are agitated with the guns out, the vague shape already de-forming, becoming darker, teeth and claws beginning to form. "Put the guns down." Everyone obeys silently. This is why I wanted to find him first; my team may be loyal like nothing else, but they're all trigger happy when they're nervous.

And everyone here is pretty nervous.

The shadows take a better shape. A man made of shadows and wind, almost my age, stands before me, empty black eyes boring into my soul.

"Hey Roger," I say, holding out a hand. A shadow hand is put in mine, more solid than the shape before. More human. "I promised I'd come for you, didn't I?"

"**AaVaA**." He croaks and nods happily. I turn to see my team.

"Everyone. I'd like you to meet Roger. My older brother."

KEEN AND KEEN INC.

DAMON WAS THROWING HIS small knife up in the air and catching it between his fingers repeatedly when there was a knock at the small street-level apartment he and his sister Cora shared.

"Damon!" Cora called, like the corner Damon always sat in was on the other side of the world. "Get the door if you would."

She did not look up from the mountain of paperwork in front of her, much less at the door.

Damon scowled. When they were younger, he would have snapped back with something dripped in sarcasm, but after what the two of them had dubbed "the incident" his throat had been split almost from ear to ear.

The scar was still there, and Cora had told him that he had been lucky: his vocal cords were very thoroughly severed but he had lived.

Damon slammed his hand down on his desk, which made Cora turn her head to look at him with her eyebrow raised.

Damon signed:

Get the damn door yourself for once

"It's 'for once, could you get the damn door.' Really, Damon, did the Army teach you anything useful?"

Damon just flipped her off and went to the door.

His job was to intimidate any prospective clients that came to Keen & Keen Inc., so he stood to his full height, which almost reached the top of the doorway, and made sure to scowl when he opened the door.

Keen & Keen Inc. had been in business for six years and had earned a reputation in this part of the city.

They were the best.

If anyone needed someone intimidated, needed information, needed something stolen, or someone or something gotten rid of, they were the ones to go to.

Their clients needed to be shown from the beginning that the two of them could be tough.

"Hey Damon!"

This was not a client.

Hello Ivy

Ivy was one of the two 16th Street witches. She was the enchanter and her partner Rose was a spellcaster. They made a good living on Ivy's pendants, potions, and other magical knickknacks, and Rose's spells to help with everything. Rose even had some spells to add some kick to Ivy's merch. Since they were so good at their job, no one minded that they were only fifteen.

Why are you here?

"We…need a favor."

What kind of favor?

"Damon?" Cora's voice drifted to the door. "Who's there?"

"Hi Ms. Cora!" Ivy said.

"Ivy!" Cora walked to the door. She was a full foot shorter than Damon but was a different type of intimidating. Especially now, since she had on her trademark white lab jacket spattered with suspicious red stains. "Well come in, come in. You have to excuse my brother; he has no manners."

Damon was about to punch her shoulder when Cora glared and said, "Damon I will stab you with a scalpel."

Ivy smiled in an attempt to keep the peace between the two that had been absent since they were five.

"I'm sure Cora wouldn't *really* stab you with a scalpel."

At the same time Damon signed, *No, she would*

Cora said, "No, I would."

Ivy briefly wondered why in the world Rose looked up to the two of the them so much but pushed the thought aside. They were siblings, chaos was part of the package.

Cora led Ivy to the small kitchen in the back. Ivy nervously sat down on one of the mismatched chairs and glared at Damon when he started to pick his teeth with one of his knives.

"Damon, can you get the cups?" Cora asked, already getting the tea water to boil with a heat stone.

Damon locked eyes with Ivy and mimicked Cora in sign but sauntered over to get the mugs. Ivy could swear Cora was rolling her eyes but she couldn't see her face.

In a minute the three of them were seated at the table with cups of tea and Cora said:

"So, what brings you to our humble establishment? I'm guessing it wasn't for conversation."

"Ah, no. I need a favor. Like a big favor."

Damon and Cora shared a look.

"Like 'hide a body' big?"

Or like bribe multiple officials for proper documentation to keep your business running?

"Smuggling a dragon?"

Okay now I don't care what it is, I just want to smuggle a dragon

"You could barely smuggle yourself in a wooden box."

Really? Now?

"No, nothing like that." Ivy assured them, but if anything, they looked disappointed that it wasn't more challenging.

"Then…what?"

Ivy inhaled and quietly considered giving them both some free charms in exchange. Even though they both owed her and Rose for giving them quick acids, truth serums, or other moderately illegal potions, she was asking a lot.

"Rose and I have had some very interesting clients of late—"

You need them killed

"Damon, no!" Ivy said. "No, they're nice and they pay well but Rose and I will have to do a very intense spell and we will need three days to prepare it. In the meantime, I need you to…look after their brother."

Silence.

We're not babysitters

Cora said, "Well I babysit you quite a lot but—no, in a professional capacity, we are not babysitters."

Ivy gulped. Cora had a light attitude now but that could turn remarkably quickly.

"This is why this is a favor. You guys owe us a lot, but I'm willing to throw a few more charms in too."

Why us? If you needed the kid out of the way there are a bunch of other ways to do it

"The child was the prisoner of a necromancer for three years and that necromancer is sending minions after him. The spell we will perform will shield the child from the necromancer and our clients will do what they will."

"So, they'll kill the necromancer when they get the chance."

"I don't discuss client's matters outside of the business."

Cora and Damon looked at each other and had what probably amounted to a three-hour debate in a few raised eyebrows and nods in roughly three seconds.

"How old is this child?"

Ivy tried not to let the relief she felt bleed onto her face. "Ten."

When can we expect the charms by?

"Eight tomorrow. I'll bring the kid then, too."

"Guess we'll have to childproof the place a bit." Cora hummed. "Same type of charms?"

"Luck, protection, recovery, and health. Same old."

Cora smiled and held out her hand for Ivy to shake. Ivy did not stare at the stains on her coat.

"Well then Ivy. You have yourself a deal."

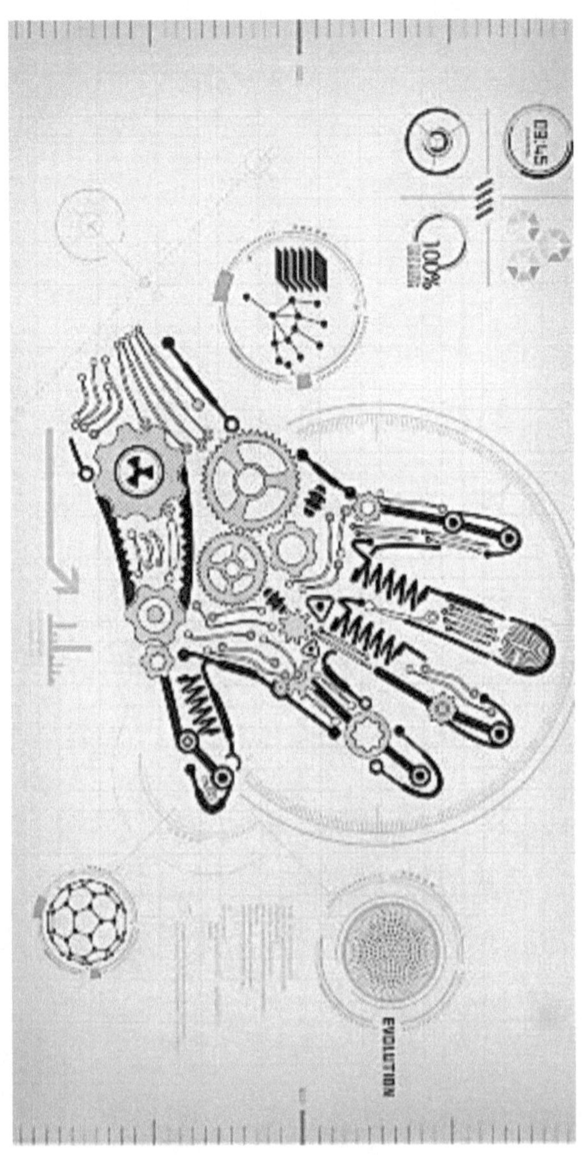

A CLOSET FULL OF KILLER ROBOTS

SILVER STEPPED DOWN THE wooden stairs gingerly. Even though Sol Lotus had been remodeled to an almost futuristic standpoint, the basement stairs were still wood, still old, and still creaked. They marked the beginning of the massive labyrinth of tunnels that the city of New York had somehow okayed.

Silver flicked the light switch at the bottom out of tradition and, true to form, it crackled, then didn't work. He flicked on his flashlight, adjusted his bag, and made a beeline for the door on the right. Tobias had said that there were some materials they needed to calm Xotol down after he had had a particularly nasty flashback. Xotol's powers had gone haywire, the lights in his room blew out, and he set his bed on fire. They had to call Grannus in to fix it.

Grannus and Qi were still calming Xotol down and Silver was sent to get a very specific type of medicine from the basement. Qi had given him very specific, if hushed, instructions to get to the right room. It was odd that she told him like it was a huge secret. She had acted like that before when Silver didn't know that the "mental patients" of Sol Lotus were actually superpowered lab rats who went out to do morally questionable things around the world.

But he knew that now. The Doctor had told him and okayed him staying there if he didn't tell anyone. So why was Qi acting so odd?

Silver tried to push it out of his mind as he went down the dark corridor. There were doors on all sides of him, padlocked or boarded up and all Silver could hear was his own heartbeat. He stepped in front of a dusty door labeled "R:1 – R:18". That was the right door, at least according to Qi. He very carefully pulled open the door with a horrible creaking sound—and almost screamed.

There were robots there.

Six rows of three, neatly lined up and powered down. There were a few smaller ones that looked a bit like miniature tanks with faces, and more that looked like smaller versions of The Iron Giant, and one right in front, half-blackened with fire, that looked almost human. Because it couldn't be human, Silver told himself. It can't be.

There was a pill bottle hanging from their neck with Qi's neat handwriting on the label: *"Sorry you had to find out this way. Maybe one day we'll wake Galataea up, but not now. Hurry back."*

Silver took the bottle with shaking hands and closed the door. He didn't think about how Galataea seemed to move when his fingers brushed their neck.

This place was weird enough.

ORIGIN

AND

DANDELION

Where… am I?

You have begun

Who are you?

My name is of no import

Name…what's my name?

Also, of no import

I—I'm on a cay. A very small cay.

Yes

Why do I know I'm on a cay? Why do I know what a cay is but not my own name?

It is of no import

Then what **is** of import?

Getting food, getting shelter

Why is it so cold?

Look across the water

There's a main shore across the water. With trees covered in snow. Do I need to go there?

If you so desire

Is there food there? Is there shelter there?

You must find that on your own

I…have to swim to the next cay. I can see it. I have to swim to that cay and then I can swim to the main shore. It's too far to swim in one go.

Correct

There's a bag on the ground. How did it get here?

It is of no import

Is it mine? If it has something inside is it mine?

If you so wish

Bread. It has bread inside. I eat bread, don't I?

It is food

There's a dead fish in here. Salmon, but I can't eat it until I've cooked it, I could get sick.

Correct

There are matches, I use matches to start a fire. I use fire to cook, and to see.

Those are some of fire's uses

There's an axe. It's new isn't it?

It has been made recently yes

I use axes to chop wood and to protect myself.

Those are some of axes' uses

There's a jacket in here. It's for the cold isn't it?

Correct

Do I put it on?

If you so wish

Jackets are clothes, aren't they?

Correct

There are other clothes in here, but they aren't jackets.

They are not

What are they? Is that at least of import?

You have a shirt, you have pants, you have socks and shoes

Socks and shoes go on my feet, they protect me from the ground. Pants and shirts protect me from the weather.

Correct

Should I put the clothes on before or after I swim?

That is your decision

The clothes will get wet in the sea, won't they?

They will

If I keep the clothes in the bag, will the bag keep them dry?

It will

Should I bring the bag with me? Should I put everything back inside before I swim? I can put the clothes on after I swim.

If you so wish

I'm going to.

That is your decision

The water is cold!

Temperature affects all things

Why do I know how to swim? Why do I know what bags are and what bread and axes are but not my name?

It is of no import

Why can't I remember anything before waking up here?

Focus on swimming, there are things in the water you don't want to see and you don't want them to see you

There are monsters.

Yes

They are ancient.

They can be

I'll focus until we reach the next cay.

That is your decision

What's this on the next cay's edge? It's not sand, it's not dirt, it's not water. Is it water?

If the temperature is low enough water will freeze into ice

It's slippery. How to I climb it?

Use your arms and your core

That takes strength, doesn't it? Why can I do it?

That is of no import

I'm going to rest here for a minute, and then I'll swim to the mainland.

Very well

Why is my throat hurting?

You're thirsty

I need water.

Correct

Not sea water though. I can't drink sea water.

Correct

I need to get to the mainland and find water.

Water is necessary for survival, yes

My bag is dry enough. It's much less of a swim to the mainland now, I can mostly stay on the ice. I don't want to be wet and cold, do I?

You do not

I'll get sick?

Correct

But a different sick than if I ate the salmon without cooking it.

A different sickness, yes

I'm going to swim to the ice. Should I concentrate here too?

It is your decision

Are there monsters this close to shore?

Not in the day

I think I'll still concentrate anyway.

That is your decision

What was that sound?

The ice is cracking, but you are close enough to shore, so you'll be okay

Snow. Snow is different from ice. I'm standing on snow now and not ice.

Correct

Are they similar as well?

Yes, if the temperature is low enough in the water ice forms, if the temperature is low enough in the sky, snow will fall

Rain usually falls from the sky.

Correct

It helps crops grow. I can drink rain.

You can indeed

Can I drink snow?

Yes, but don't drink snow from the ground, wait for it to fall

I've put on the shirt and the pants and the socks and the shoes. I don't feel as cold now.

That is what clothes are for

I want to keep walking farther in. This many trees means that it is a forest, right?

Correct

Is that red thing an apple?

Yes

Can I take it?

If you so desire

Okay, then. What is that? A small tree?

A flower

What type?

A dandelion

Can I take it with me?

Plants need soil, water, and air to live

But can I take it with me?

You could take it with you but you would have to kill it

I don't want to kill it.

That is your decision

Where do dandelions come from?

Their seeds

The seeds are planted and then they have water, and air, and then they live?

Correct

Where are their seeds stored?

In the white wisps

Where do **I** come from?

It is of no import

Was I planted?

You were not

Can dandelions grow where it is so cold?

These ones can

I'm going to take some of the seeds with me. I'll put the jacket on and put the seeds inside and then I'll plant them somewhere.

That is your decision

I'm going to do it.

Very well

I feel even less cold with the jacket. What is it made of?

Nylon and water repellent polyester

I like it.

That is your decision

How long have I been walking through this forest?

Two hours

I'm hungry. If I'm hungry I should eat right?

Correct

I'll have the bread while I walk.

That is your decision

I'm going to do it.

Very well

What's that? Are they odd trees? I know this, don't I?

You do

They're…buildings.

Correct

It's a village!

Correct

I can get food here, and shelter, and supplies!

Correct

There are people here. I—I'm people, too, aren't I?

If you choose to be

I'm different from them, aren't I?

Yes

Why?

It is of no import

Are they friendly? That one is looking at me.

These villagers are friendly, yes

I greet people, don't I?

It is customary

Hello! Why are they walking away?

They did not hear you

But I spoke…HELLO! Why won't they answer? What are they saying to each other? Why don't I understand them? Why are their mouths moving when they speak?

One question at a time

Their throats are moving, they—they're making noises with their throats. Why can't I do that? Can I speak?

You are speaking to me

You—you're in my mind!

Correct

They don't talk with their minds?

No

Why can't I talk with them? **Why won't my throat work!**

Touch your throat

Why?

To find out why

It's…uneven? The skin is slightly raised along the middle. What is that?

Scar tissue

Scars…heal over wounds, right?

Correct

My throat…was injured and now I can only talk with my mind.

Correct

How was my throat damaged?

It is of no import

Why is it of no import?

It does not impede your ability to find food or find shelter

I can only talk with you?

There are ways to communicate with your hands, with gestures and with writing

Can you teach me to speak with my hands?

You already know how, but I will help you remember

Will they understand me if I talk with my hands?

Not all of them, but they will understand if you write

Alright…what do I do?

Find a house to sleep in

There will be beds. I sleep in beds, don't I?

Correct

That building looks empty, should we go in?

That is your decision

I'm doing it.

Very well

This is a nice building, isn't it? The bed is comfortable and there is a place to put my bag.

It is well constructed

There was a sign outside to trade. What's trade?

You give someone a good or service that they want and they give you a good or service you want

The villagers outside were writing things down. I need something to write on, don't I?

It would be an easier way to communicate yes

What do I write on?

There is paper to write on in a notebook

Will you show me what a notebook is if the someone I am trading with has one?

I will

I'm going to go trade. It's my decision, isn't it?

Correct

I'm doing it. Very well?

Very well

What is all of this? Is this all part of trade?

They are items that people want

Is there a notebook?

Yes, the object with leather wrapped around paper on the left side of the counter

How do I tell this person I want it?

Point to it

I can't answer what he's saying. I don't understand what he's saying!

He says that it will be a food item

Oh. I still have the apple. Do I hold it out to him?

Correct

He took it.

Then you can take the notebook

 It's getting dark. I don't want to be outside when it's dark, right?

Correct

There are monsters.

Correct

They can't get in though, right?

Not if you lock your door

The door?

The large piece of wood you passed when you went inside; shut that and the monsters stay out

I'll do it. I want to go back to the building. It is my decision, right?

It is

And if I say "I'm doing it" you'll say "very well."

I will

I'm doing it.

Very well

The door is shut, the light is on, but I'm not tired yet.

Then do not sleep yet

The trader gave me an odd stick, too.

It is a pencil, you use it to write

Very well. On the first page I should write who I am, so I can introduce myself.

Very well

But I don't have a name. Do I have a name?

Yes

What is it? Can't you tell me?

It is of no import

Everything and everyone has a name, though.

Correct

Then I need a name.

Very well

Can I pick a name?

You can

The seeds are still in my pocket…I'll call myself Dandelion.

Very well Dandelion

You need a name too. I know you said your name was of no import but it must be. You always identify things to me by their name. Names are important, aren't they?

They are an identity

But are they **important**?

They can be

You said I was beginning. What's beginning?

A start, a first part, an origin

Origin! I can call you Origin!

What

That'll be your name! You've always been with me since the beginning so you'll be my origin, Origin!

You are going to call me Origin?

If you won't tell me your real name, then yes.

Very well Dandelion

There's the first page then! Hello, my name is Dandelion and I'm traveling with Origin. There, it's done.

People will think you're crazy if that's how you introduce yourself

What's crazy?

Never mind, just go to sleep and I'll tell you in the morning

All right… goodnight Origin.

Goodnight Dandelion

We

Few

Old

Souls

"Each night, when I go to sleep, I die. And the next morning... I am reborn."

– Gandhi

HOLLY FOUND DAMIEN IN the thistles in the courtyard at three in the morning. Again. The reason Holly had even left her small apartment and her loyal husky Faulkner at the devil's hour was because the fire alarm in the building had blared at a volume that seemed to rival a jet engine. Holly had looked outside and had seen no fire, had smelled no smoke, but suspected who had tripped the alarm that had the rest of the complex up in arms. So she had pulled on her brother's old bomber jacket and rushed down the back stairs.

And found Damien in the thistles in nothing but his undershorts and socks staring up at the cold winter sky.

"Damien, what are you doing out here?"

"Looking for life in the stars. What are *you* doing out here, Holly?"

"Get out of the thistles, we have to find Pearl."

A dramatic sigh. "*Must* we? I do have such a lovely view of the stars."

"…There are no stars out tonight Damien. There are clouds over the entire sky."

A shrug.

Holly pinched her brow and looked at the surrounding windows that still had lights in them. "Fine then. *I'll* find Pearl but you're getting out of these bushes when we come back."

"A sound compromise."

Holly found Pearl exactly where she thought she would be: squatting under the fire alarm with a burnt-out match. That match seemed to be the last one she had lit; there were at least five more scattered around.

Holly stopped the girl before she reached for a fresh one. Pearl was in her snowflake pajamas that she had gotten a year ago for her eleventh birthday and wasn't wearing her slippers.

"Pearl. Let's go."

The girl looked up at her with huge brown eyes. "Why?"

"It's freezing out here—"

"Hence the matches."

"Which you decided to burn under literally the only fire alarm outside. At three in the morning."

"I was worried that one of them was getting out of control and I didn't want anyone hurt." Pearl pointed to one of the burnt-out matches that was burned all the way to the stub and completely blackened.

Holly sat down next to her. "Did you burn yourself with that one?"

Pearl nodded without looking away from the dead matches on the stone ground. "I'm usually far more careful. A pity."

"Let's clean these up, okay? You need to be getting home."

"My home is far too loud. Even at three in the morning."

"You aren't coming over to my place. Your mother already doesn't like me."

"My mother doesn't like anyone but her plants. And I want to see Faulkner."

Holly pinched her brow again and held out her hand. "Extra matches and lighters. I know you have them."

Pearl reluctantly handed over her silver lighter and box of 100 matches. They buried the burnt matches in the dirt and walked back to the thistles.

Damien looked almost angelic wrapped in the thistles, with his eyes gently closed, no longer looking at the sky.

"Damien," Holly said, "let's go."

Damien simply held out his arm, already bristling with prickles. Holly winced with empathy, gently took his hand, and pulled him forward.

The three of them went up to Holly's apartment in silence and Faulkner was there to greet them.

Pearl curled up with Faulkner in front of the (unlit) oven with a dog-eared copy of Holly's *Fahrenheit 451*. Holly had put a quick coat of Noxema on the tip of her finger and a band-aid over it. Holly started painstakingly taking out the prickles from Damien's body, first out of his legs and shorts so he could sit down to do the rest.

At about 3:25 Holly said, "Pearl, can you get the extra band-aids from the bathroom?"

Pearl retrieved them without a word and Faulkner retrieved his favorite toy, a blue carrot, and placed it at Damien's feet, wagging his tail all the while. Faulkner enthusiastically received his head scritches and in his enthusiasm jostled a few prickles in Damien's arm.

"Faulkner," Holly said, "lie down."

Faulkner curled up at Damien's feet while Holly used her tweezers to their fullest extent and placed each plucked thorn in a waiting bowl of water. Pearl would then wipe the area with rubbing alcohol and place a bright blue band-aid over the wound.

Damien was silent for most of the ordeal, on occasion hissing when the rubbing alcohol was too roughly applied or the thorn too quickly removed. At about 4:30 he said, "It's far too quiet."

All other residents of the small apartment glared at him with tired eyes. But Holly turned on her phone and selected Damien's favorite book anyway.

"No one would have believed in the last years of the nineteenth century that this world was being watched keenly and closely by intelligences greater than man's and yet as mortal as his own."

Damien relaxed then, and the prickles seemed to come out more easily. Pearl yawned and after both Damien's arms had been cleared of thistles Holly put on a strong pot of coffee.

"That as men busied themselves about their various concerns they were scrutinised and studied…"

All three of them drank their coffee while they worked: Pearl all at once, savoring the burn in her throat, Holly with a rhythm, take out a prickle, sip while Pearl was applying a band-aid, lather rinse repeat. Damien sipped his carefully. Although his arms were clear, his back was still a work in progress and his arms were in a bit of pain.

"…perhaps almost as narrowly as a man with a microscope might scrutinise the transient creatures that swarm and multiply in a drop of water."

It was almost six in the morning when every prickle had been removed, when the coffee pot had been filled and emptied three times, when Faulkner had drifted into a soft slumber, when they could finally rest.

"With infinite complacency men went to and fro over this globe about their little affairs, serene in their assurance of their empire over matter."

It was seven in the morning when Nicolas opened the door with his spare key. He had brought a box of doughnuts and more coffee. None of them believed there was such a thing as "too much coffee."

"Hey everyone! How did you sleep last night?" He knew that if any of them had been over to Holly's that sleep was the last thing that would happen, but manners were manners.

The scene that was presented to him was this: Damien was fast asleep on his stomach on Holly's old green vinyl couch covered in so many band-aids there was hardly any Damien left; Pearl was asleep on the floor in an odd contorted position; and Holly had fallen asleep at her post, in the chair next to the couch with Faulkner at her feet.

They all stirred to some sort of consciousness with the smell of baked goods and the intrusion of light in their secluded lair.

"Bless you Nicolas," Holly mumbled with a doughnut in her mouth. Pearl was still asleep and Damien wasn't hungry yet, content to listen to *The War of the Worlds* some more.

Nicolas smiled. "Anytime."

And thus, a brand new day began.

"The flower that follows the sun
does so even in cloudy days."
– Robert Leighton

DAMIEN WAS OUT OF HOLLY'S apartment before sunrise. It had been three weeks since his unfortunate incident with the thistles, and the stubborn wounds had finally healed. Holly probably would have shot him less worried looks if he hadn't had another "incident" the week before.

Damien was wearing Holly's sneakers and the bomber jacket since she wasn't awake yet and he figured she wouldn't mind.

Damien ran his hand along the stone walls of the complex and hummed *Mademoiselle from Armentieres* under his breath as he walked into town.

The streets were still foggy as the light of the sun hadn't quite penetrated yet. Not that Damien minded. He loved everything about foggy weather: the cold, the fact that one could get lost in one's own private bubble of cloud, the silence.

Which is when a firetruck came speeding down the street blaring its horn so loudly that Damien couldn't hear himself think. He vaguely wondered if Pearl had started a huge fire but dismissed the idea. She was far too careful with her controlled burns to ever let them get out of hand. The incident a few weeks prior was simply a fluke.

Damien walked to the flower shop that was always open early and knocked on the door. Bella, the owner, put down her phone, took out her air pods, opened the door for him and smiled.

"Good morning Damien." She paused. "Do I want to know what happened to your arm?"

Damien looked down at the dark blue cast that covered his right forearm. Holly, Pearl, and Nicolas had all signed it with a bright pink sharpie Pearl had taken from her sister. Damien shrugged. "I had a very unfortunate accident last week. Not to worry, Holly's making me take good care of it, she's even kind enough to put the blow drier on cold and blow air into it when my skin gets irritated, and she always makes sure I raise my arm above my heart, so whenever the bugger starts swelling it will stop."

Bella raised an eyebrow. Not much excited her these days, but Damien's stupid antics were always interesting.

"Speaking of Holly," Bella said, "isn't that Michael's jacket?"

"Yes."

"Literally her most treasured possession in the world that's not Faulkner?"

"Indeed."

"And she let you wear it?"

"She doesn't know I have it."

"So, you stole it?"

"I'm giving it back when I get home. I'm *borrowing* it."

Which is when another customer walked in. Before he could

say a word, Bella held up her hand with her eyes still on Damien.

"Roses in the corner are on sale just get those."

The man was about to speak, but Bella was quicker.

"No, you don't need to pay me. Just take them and get out."

The man left with a bouquet of roses without a word. Bella focused her attention again on Damien and brought her Starbucks back to her mouth.

"How did you break your arm?"

"Jumped out of a moving car."

"Really?" A sip. "How fast was the car going?"

"Oh…maybe 20. I landed on quite a bit of vegetation though, so I just broke my arm in a few places."

"Why did you jump?"

"My driver was very much getting on my nerves, so I decided to get out early."

Bella laughed at that. "How did Holly find out?"

"Good Samaritan."

Bella raised her eyebrow at that and Damien pulled out his wallet. On top of his ID was a handwritten note with Holly's signature cursive reading, *If this man did something stupid and is now hurt and/or in trouble with the law please call this number…*

Bella laughed even harder at that. She usually laughed softly, the picture of grace and privilege, but the note had her laughing until she snorted.

The two of them talked for a bit more, and Bella gave Damien a beautiful bouquet of chrysanthemums in full bloom for free and Damien headed home, feeling light on his feet.

He hummed as he knocked on Holly's door. There were sounds of rummaging and muffled cursing inside.

"Who is it?" Holly's voice came through the door.

"It's me. I have a present."

Holly opened the door, looking haggard and stressed. Then in a very, very low very, very dangerous voice said,

"Damien?"

"Yes?"

"Why. Do you. Have. My. Jacket?"

"It was really cold out—"

"Damien! You know damn well what that jacket means to— Are those my sneakers?"

"Oh. Yeah, sorry, mine have holes in them. But I got you flowers?"

"Flowers? You stole my shoes—"

"Borrowed."

"You *stole* my shoes and Mi-my jacket to get me *flowers?*"

"They're chrysanthemums though."

"I don't give a damn if they're solid gold, Damien! I put up with a lot—a lot of your shit and—"

"Which is exactly why I got you these. Chrysanthemums symbolize thanks for a good friend."

Silence. Holly pinched her brow, and the anger was gone from her voice. She just sounded tired: "Give me my jacket back Damien."

"That will be a bit difficult what with the broken arm and

holding the flowers."

Holly snatched the flowers and promptly hit Damien across the face with them before setting them gently on a stack of books inside the door.

Damien rubbed his cheek. "I deserved that, didn't I?"

"You did." She held out her hand. "The jacket."

Damien struggled out of the jacket and handed it to her. He didn't miss the look of relief that washed over her face when she put it back on.

"…Can I come in?"

Holly sighed deeply. "Yes Damien you can come in." Damien followed her in the door. "Just take off my sneakers when you come in, don't wake Faulkner, Nick's bringing coffee and doughnuts in an hour, Pearl's probably coming over later…"

Damien had taken off the shoes and had gathered the chrysanthemums to put in water when Holly turned around and said, "Damien?"

"Yes."

"If you ever take my jacket without my permission again, I will end you. And they will never find your body. Understood?"

Damien nodded three times, "Understood." He knew of and quite believed Patrick Rothfuss's quote about wise men fearing three things, the chief among them being the anger of a gentle man.

Damien had seen Holly furious before, and he had no desire to see that again. He promised himself not to take her jacket even if he was freezing to death. Her sneakers were still fair game, though.

*"From time to time, there arise among human beings
people who seem to exude love as naturally
as the sun gives out heat"* – Alan Watts

REBEL BLINKED BACK TO life on a hospital gurney and it slowly dawned on them that this wasn't the first time.

They had been in the hospital a few times before of course, once with a broken arm and the other with pneumonia they got from staying out all night in the rain.

But this was different. Rebel squinted from the glare of the light and listened to the relieved sounds of the doctors. But they weren't the right doctors.

It slowly dawned on Rebel that it wasn't a doctor speaking, it was a friend. The friend was speaking French, which Rebel had never understood but suddenly the odd flowing words started to make sense. Rebel was still blinded by the light when the voice said,

"Ralph! Stay with me okay? They're going to take good care of you."

Rebel thought that they knew that voice. "Rebel," they tried to rasp through the respirator, "Rebel, not Ralph."

Rebel was then suddenly aware that there was a searing pain in their throat and lungs, like they had swallowed fire, and they were aware that it wasn't because of the light that they couldn't see right, their eyes were burning too.

Rebel screamed and screamed. They screamed until the doctors had to sedate them and sleep pulled them gently down into an inky blackness.

Rebel dreamed so much, but none of it felt like a dream. It felt like they were remembering.

"Rachel what are you doing here you could be killed!" It was a man dressed in military blue who spoke, and gunfire whizzed from nearby. Rebel found themselves—or Rachel answering,

"This is my war too Henry. Give me a gun and pants, I'll drive them out of Gettysburg myself if you won't." Gettysburg. Rebel knew that it was a battle in the American Civil War but they had fallen asleep in history class for that and had gotten every question wrong on the test.

But now, through Rachel's eyes, Rebel saw the slaughter, heard the screams, and somehow knew all about the 1860's. Everything got faster and faster, Rebel flew through light tunnels and saw so much it made their head hurt.

They saw themselves, swimming desperately at Dunkirk, in the trenches in the Somme, then further and further back. They were running through Edo in the 1770's, then celebrating the birth of Maharana Udai Singh in the 1520's. Earlier and earlier and faster and faster until Rebel's brain hurt.

Then everything paused. All at once. Rebel was floating in the same inky darkness and tried to catch their breath. Then they felt the tug.

Rebel had been feeling the odd tug ever since they were a child, the sense to just go a certain direction, that something was missing, that they had to find *something* but they never knew what.

But now it was clearer, a dull throb that was responded to by more throbs from the blackness. Rebel wasn't sure what to do until they heard themselves from the darkness, over and over in a hundred different languages, a thousand times but still saying the same thing:

"We—we're connected somehow. Our souls are bound together and every time the last of us dies we start to be reborn, not all at once but we start. And every time we find each other, across continents and across oceans because we have to."

Rebel's soul throbbed and so did the responses.

"How do you know?" a voice asked, in a hundred languages and a thousand times.

"I died. I died and I remembered everything. I remembered all of you. Don't you all just feel off sometimes? Like there should be more you remember? That something fundamental is missing from your life but you don't know what? That it almost seems like you're from a different time?"

Silence. And then:

"By the Gods."

"God in heaven."

"Holy shit!"

Rebel saw the voices come to life. Saw themselves telling six or seven people the same thing throughout the centuries. In temples, on boats, dying in bed, over and over and over.

Rebel was only terrified for a moment, before all of the memories came rushing back. Rebel reasoned that they themselves were effectively immortal. Even after death, Rebel would just come back and remember.

The voices started to quiet and the darkness started to recede. Rebel slowly blinked open their eyes to see the worried faces of the doctors and their parents.

There was only one thought in Rebel's mind then, and they knew it had been there thousands of times before: *I have to find them.*

Rebel was almost fifteen when they had been stupid enough to fall off their parents' house and end up in the hospital. They were sixteen when they found the rest of the souls.

The summer before going to their new boarding school was the quietest Rebel had ever been. They didn't run around, didn't stay up until 5 in the morning playing *Assassin's Creed*, didn't find new ways to be almost caught by the police. They just lay in bed and remembered.

And there was quite a lot to remember. Rebel's parents were so worried that the two of them had Rebel taken to a psychologist, who pronounced Rebel perfectly sane even though Rebel didn't feel anywhere close to it.

They knew almost 50 languages now, although quite a few were antiquated or very dead. They had read over 1,000 books which was nothing really compared to the other souls they were going to find. At least two of them always read voraciously, and it was highly possible the two of them had read a good third of all books ever written.

Rebel looked on the internet like someone possessed for one of the souls, the one who the others tended to gather around. Rebel had always tended to drive the other souls away. They pored over social media, newspapers, college yearbooks just looking, knowing they would know when they saw the soul.

They remembered a previous life, where they had been stillborn but brought back and had always known. They remembered how they had attuned their soul to find the others, and they used that skill again.

It was the 3rd of August when Rebel found her: *Haruaki, Hanna, Henry, Hardouin, Hedi…*

Holly. Her name was Holly Green, she was twenty-six years old, graduated from the University of Glasgow, and lived a whole three blocks from their new school.

She had almost no presence online but Rebel was able to find another soul named Bella whose story was full of pictures of the group. There were pictures of the five of them—Rebel learned that the other souls were going by Pearl, Damien, and Nicolas—at a diner early in the morning, all in the park, playing with a husky, drinking hot cider at Christmas…

Rebel's concentration was almost broken when the ice cream truck came down the lane but they resisted the urge to chase after it. Rebel's mother was especially concerned with this, since Rebel ran after the truck all the time; on one memorable occasion, with a twisted ankle.

But where was the seventh? There had always been seven souls since the beginning of time, but that soul was nowhere to be found. Rebel felt their stomach sink when they realized that they couldn't feel the soul anywhere in the world.

Looking back, there had only ever been five other tugs at their soul. When had the seventh died? It had to be at least the same year Rebel was born. Rebel stayed up until three in the morning looking at obituaries from the time the last soul died in 1989 to Rebel's birth year.

Rebel found the soul in a newspaper clipping dated four months before they were born that just read: *Local teen tragically dead in DUI: sister said he "seemed off lately."*

Rebel read the article all the way through. Since it was a small town, there were quite a few details: interviews with teachers, friends, and family. They all said that he had always seemed so miserable, even when he was a child, but that he was a good person and they were so sad to lose him.

His yearbook photo was included and Rebel could have sworn they had seen the face before. They strained their brain but they were so tired that they fell asleep right there, with the soul still looking at them.

Rebel was jittery the week before school started, triple checking everything, making sure they had all the documentation they could get on everyone's previous lives to help convince them.

They barely slept.

When school finally started Rebel waited all week to get a pass to go to the city that first weekend. They were so anxious a teacher had to take them out to the hall to make sure they weren't having a panic attack.

But thanks to all the knowledge they had from previous lives, Rebel was doing a lot better in school and was granted a pass even though the principal really thought they should take a buddy.

The first weekend, Rebel was almost hit by two cars when they made a mad dash across a street since they had a full three seconds left on the crosswalk. The tugs were getting stronger and stronger as they neared the small apartment complex that the rest of the souls were in.

They dashed around all four floors of the apartment building. There were names on each door in fine black print and Rebel knocked frantically on the first one that said Green.

It opened an inch.

"Hi, are you Holly Green?"

The door slammed in their face. Guess not.

They ran to the second and third floor which had no Greens and onto the fourth. They saw a woman with her back to them with an old bomber jacket stepping out of her apartment to lock it, a husky squirming at her legs.

Rebel didn't even need to see the name on the apartment. Their soul just sang with joy.

"HOLLY!" Rebel yelled, running forward.

"Shit!" She yelled, dropping the keys. Rebel ran forward to hug their friend when they tripped over their own shoes and heard their nose go *crunch* on the concrete. Not that it stopped them. Rebel had a broken nose, a bruise on their head, and they were crying but it didn't matter. Holly was *here!*

"Shit! Kid, are you okay?" Holly said, rushing forward. Rebel tried to stand but found their lap full of a husky licking their face.

"I found you," they whispered. Holly leaned down to check Rebel's forehead and Rebel just hugged her tight. They hadn't seen her in almost forty years, after all.

"Heh, yeah kid. You found me. You also really need to clean up that nose—"

"Holly? You okay?" A voice drifted through the open door, it sounded like there was a cough in that throat and a girl who couldn't be more than twelve came to the door, wrapped in a blanket.

"Pearl!" Rebel yelled, but when they tried to run to their friend, Holly held their arm.

"Okay kid you need to calm down."

"But you're here! You're all *here* I can feel it. I-I have to tell you. I have to show you!"

Holly looked very concerned for their sanity. Rebel couldn't blame her.

"I think you need to come inside okay kid?" Holly asked. "I'll get you cleaned up and then I'll call your school—"

"No need!" Rebel said quickly. They couldn't endanger any future passes.

"Okay…" Holly said still holding their arm. "Can you stand?" Rebel nodded so vigorously that blood spewed from their nose and Holly winced.

Rebel was led inside where Damien and Nicolas were fighting to the death in *Mario Kart* and Bella was scrolling through her phone on a chair, bored as could be. Pearl walked back over to the couch and flopped down grabbing at the nearby tissues.

"Holly, you have a bleeding heart," Damien said, not looking away from the screen.

"Mm, kid has a bleeding face," she responded. Rebel was sat down and soon their nose was no longer bleeding and a compress was on their head.

"So, what did you mean by 'we're all here'?" Holly asked after the game had finished. The five of them were watching Rebel in the same way they always had, wondering why they were so drawn to them.

"It's a long story." Rebel said, "And it was much easier to tell you all this when most of you were Buddhist." They received five raised eyebrows. "You aren't going to believe me. Not at first, you never do, Nicolas you're going to ask how I know and you always do and I'll tell you I've died and remembered, I always do."

Bella actually took her air pods out to listen to what Rebel said next. No one laughed, it seemed like no one even breathed because Rebel knew that in the back of all of their minds was some memory that was making itself known. Some feeling that they could never place, a dream they had no way of knowing…

Rebel took a deep breath and said for the thousandth time, "We—we're connected somehow. Our souls are bound together and every time the last of us dies we start to be reborn, not all at once but we start. And every time we find each other, across continents and across oceans because we have to."

"Christmas is the day that holds all time together"

– Alexander Smith

REBEL RAN THEIR HANDS over the carved wooden reindeer on Holly's windowsill. Some things never changed.

Holly had had a deep connection with this time of year throughout all of her lives, from celebrating the wild hunt with glee, to somehow sneaking an entire Yule log into the trenches and playing football with the Germans.

Rebel was very cozy with their red turtleneck, watching the snow softly fall, and holding a cup of warm cider when Holly came back through her apartment door with Faulkner in tow.

"Rebel, come on we're all going to the river."

"Is Faulkner coming?"

"Of course Faulkner is coming."

"Fuck yeah!" Rebel yelled and ran for the door only to be stopped by Holly's arm on their chest.

"Get your jacket on."

"Why?"

"Because it's one degree above freezing."

"I call that brisk!"

"I call that a risk of hypothermia and a trip to the hospital."

"Tomato tomato."

"Put your damn jacket on or I won't bring Faulkner."

Rebel threw on their parka and trapper hat and jumped out the door into the snow on the landing. They ran down the stairs with a yapping Faulkner behind them.

They dashed across the street at breakneck speed and ignored an irritated car horn. Rebel then promptly flopped in the snow and started to make snow angels.

"Rebel!" Holly snapped when she and Faulkner crossed the street, safely, "You could've been killed!"

Rebel shrugged, "And I will be brought back to life when the last one of you dies."

"That doesn't matter. You're alive now and you need to stay that way, okay?"

Rebel was silent for a second, making aggressive snow angels.

"Pearl!"

They jumped up and ran to the small bridge over the river where Pearl was waiting and throwing lighted matches over the railing into the freezing river, watching them fade out.

Holly pinched her brow when Rebel ran off. Faulkner snuffled around her legs; at least someone here was willing to be reasonable.

A deep and bored sigh came from Holly's right and her nose was suddenly filled with sweetened coffee.

"Hey Bella."

"Hey. Is Damien here?"

"Somewhere, probably. He and Nicolas are coming soon with hot chocolate."

"Mm."

"Oh, come on Bella, it's beautiful."

"It's *snow*. Snow is snow no matter where you are."

"But we're *here* and it's beautiful."

"Mm."

Damien and Nicolas came, bundled up, a few minutes later. Nicolas came with a cardboard tray full of hot chocolate and candy canes in his pocket.

Rebel was doing handstands on the railing of the bridge when the four of them walked up, and Holly had just drunk half her hot chocolate when Damien walked up behind her and put her in a headlock.

"Damien! What the fuck!"

"Attack of the dead men! Defend yourself!"

Holly slammed her elbow into Damien's rib cage and he stumbled back with a laugh, then tripped over Faulkner's tail and let out a quick shout before he was over the bridge railing and in the river.

Nicolas yelled, "Damien!"

Pearl snapped, "Shit!"

"We need to get down there!" Holly said.

Rebel yelled, "I'll get him!" and jumped over the rail and there was a second *splash!*

"Rebel goddammit!" Bella shouted.

The four of them ran down the bridge and were at the river's edge in a few seconds. Damien and Rebel were only ten feet away, but the cold and extra clothes made it almost impossible for them to move.

Everyone shouted. "Rebel! Damien! Keep swimming!" Faulkner barked in agreement.

Damien shouted, "My arms aren't working!"

"I'm getting my car!" Holly yelled taking Faulkner's collar.

Rebel shouted "Hurry!" as they tried to tread water towards Damien—but they couldn't reach him.

"Shit what do we do?" Bella said.

Pearl looked up from her phone and said, "Google says to pull them out with a rope, ladder, or jumper cables."

"We don't have any of those!" Bella snapped.

"We have trees. Trees have branches," Nicolas said.

Bella and Pearl rushed off to pull branches down and Nicolas stayed with the two.

"Everything's going to be okay guys! Holly's going to be back really soon and they're getting branches, so just hang in there."

"We're fucking dying Nicolas!" Rebel snapped, trying to keep their heads above the water.

"But don't worry!" Nicolas said, "Everyone will be back before you know it."

Rebel tried to glare, but the result was hardly intimidating.

Holly's old car made a screeching sound when it pulled up almost a minute later. She had blankets haphazardly thrown in the back and she opened the door with, "I'm probably getting a speeding ticket for that."

Pearl and Bella came back with some branches they'd found that succeeded in barely reaching Rebel and Damien.

"I brought rope, I brought rope," Holly said, as she got the coil from her trunk, slammed the trunk shut, ran to the river and threw the coil out.

Damien was the only one who was still partially conscious, Rebel was barely afloat and was shivering violently.

Damien tied the rope around Rebel's waist with freezing fingers and Rebel was dragged, shaking, out of the river. Bella and Pearl got them to Holly's car, where the heat was turned all the way up, and began to get Rebel out of their wet clothes and into some blankets.

"Damien!" Holly yelled; he was barely afloat. "You have to do it again, you have to tie the rope again okay?"

"What's the point really?" Damien mumbled. He had never noticed how almost peaceful the snow was, like a slowly suffocating blanket.

"Damien!" Holly said, "I-I will come in there to get you okay?"

Damien mumbled something unintelligible and let his eyes droop shut. Holly grabbed the biggest branch Bella and Pearl had broken off and tied the rope around her waist. Nicolas held onto the other end and she slowly walked onto the water.

The first foot was solid ice, but the next foot sounded like soft grinding under her feet. If the ice could barely hold her it wasn't going to hold Damien too.

"Damien! You have to reach!" She held out the branch to him. It brushed his chest but he didn't move. Then his eyes opened and he said, "You saved my life in Verdun."

"Damien grab the damn branch!"

"I was in a plane. It crashed and you pulled me out, we weren't even on the same side and you saved me."

"Damien!" Holly snapped. If his memories were coming back that meant he was close to death.

"Your name was Hardouin."

"Grab the branch!"

He grabbed the branch almost mechanically and Holly pulled him out of the freezing water with a sound like pealing thunder when the ice split. Damien grabbed Holly's jacket when he was close enough, and was about to ask if she would let him borrow it now, but the joke didn't make it past his teeth.

Nicolas was pulling them in and the second Damien was a foot from the bank Holly and Nicolas pulled him out by his coat and dragged him to the car. Rebel was wrapped in several blankets and Pearl was hugging him too.

"Can I light a fire for him?" she asked.

"No time," Holly said, already pulling Damien's clothes off. In a minute Damien was in the same cocooned state as Rebel, and Faulkner pressed close to him.

"I already called ahead to… I called ahead. They have a hospital for us. I wrote down the address," Bella said.

Holly was about to get in the front seat when Damien grabbed her arm and said, "My name was Dietrich… I had a little brother when I went away…I saw him again at Dunkirk, but I didn't know him…"

"It's okay Damien," Holly mumbled. "We'll get you to a hospital, just hold on for a minute.”

Holly drove through three red lights to get to the hospital. There were police sirens behind them after the second red light.

“Not that this is under the best of circumstances, but this is probably the most exciting thing I’ve done in a while,” Bella said, a bit breathless when Holly made a very illegal left turn.

“Glad I could make your day,” Holly said, before swerving right. “Rebel would love this.”

“ICE! HOLLY ICE!” Pearl yelled and Holly almost burned a tire tread into the road when she made a U-turn to avoid a partially frozen street.

“Bella, I got turned around,” Holly said, in an effort to keep as calm as possible with two police cars behind her. “How close are we?”

Bella checked her phone. “Uhh…damn thing’s recalibrating… wait…okay! Up this street and a hard right in three blocks.”

By now Nicolas and Pearl knew to hang on tight to Damien and Rebel when Holly came to the turn.

The sirens were deafening.

Nicolas stuck his head out the window and yelled, “HYPOTHERMIA!”

“Nicolas what the hell?” Bella asked.

“I’m sure they’ll understand,” Nicolas said.

The police did not understand Nicolas; there were three squad cars after them by the time they reached the hospital. Doctors and gurneys were waiting for them as they pulled up with a *screeeech*.

“Holy shit,” Bella said. Everyone else was breathless for a second. “Where did you learn to drive like that?”

Holly was unbuckling herself and just said, "My older brother was a daredevil. Taught me some tricks."

Pearl mumbled, "Thought it was *Mario Kart*." Faulkner licked her face and was panting but seemed to be glad the ride was over.

Nicolas wished he had the presence of mind to ask why Holly had never mentioned this brother before—not that Holly was especially close with her family—but she was already opening the side door and getting Rebel out.

The doctors took them both in on gurneys and everyone sighed in relief when the two of them were through the doors. Holly talked to the policemen and apologized for everything. They were surprisingly understanding but she was exhausted when she sat back in the car.

"Merry Christmas by the way," Bella said. Her momentary breathlessness and exhilaration at the ride were gone, replaced by her usual stone face.

Holly pinched her brow and put her head on the steering wheel. "It is Christmas, isn't it?"

"Christmas Eve, yes," Pearl said. "Did you get me presents?"

"I got everyone presents," Holly mumbled. "It'll be weird not having the two of them there."

"What if we just had Christmas in the hospital with them?" Nicolas said. "I'm sure it'll go great!"

"Sounds boring," Bella said.

Holly sighed. "Bella can you literally not. I'll go in and ask when we can see them and we'll bring the presents and everything else over." She started to unbuckle herself and turned around. "Do not mess with my car Pearl."

Pearl looked offended. "Holly! I-I am just *shocked* you would even think—"

"Nicolas don't let Pearl mess with my car."

Nicolas smiled. "Don't worry I won't!"

Holly walked back in and, after a few wrong turns, found the nurse's station and learned that it would be a few hours until Rebel and Damien would be awake enough to see visitors.

Meanwhile in the car Pearl's mind was going on a loop about Rebel. She had an itch in her fingers and the sudden urge to use the lighter in her pocket, but Holly would be incredibly angry if she burned anything in the car, like the box of Kleenex on the floor, so the lighter stayed in Pearl's pocket. She did fidget, though. She shifted to the right, then to the left and then back again. She drummed her fingers on the inside of the car in no discernible pattern. She cleared her throat four or five times and reached for her pocket but always drew away. Just making sure the lighter was there.

After two minutes of this Pearl resorted to kicking the back of the passenger seat and Bella whirled around and snapped, "Will you cut that out!"

Pearl just pouted and looked out the window. The snow had started to fall softly and Pearl watched one snowflake at a time from the first time it became visible to the time it reached the ground.

Holly came back a few minutes later.

"Well, let's get home and gather everything up. It'll be two hours until they're awake but it'll take some time to get it all together."

*   *   *

When Damien and Rebel woke up, there was a Santa Claus standing by their beds.

"The hell?" Damien rasped. Santa laughed, not a deep booming laugh but a high pealing one.

Nicolas.

Damien smiled softly, the tube in his nose half obstructing his vision.

"Merry Christmas!" Nicolas laughed. At the same time Holly, Pearl, and a reluctant Bella jumped out behind him and yelled, "Merry Christmas!"

Rebel laughed, a broken raspy thing, their lungs had taken a hard hit.

"You came back." Damien smiled.

"Of course we did," Holly said. "Spending Christmas in the hospital sucks. So, we're here to spend it with you."

"Did you bring presents?" Rebel asked.

"Of course we did," Bella said, "We were allowed to bring Faulkner in the door but he has to be in another room so he can't be here."

Rebel pouted but then said, "Did you bring candy?"

"No Rebel, you have to be on fluids for a bit," Holly said, knowing full well the doctors had told the two of them everything before they had taken a nap.

"We brought presents though!" Pearl said.

So, they all sat down until visiting hours were up and opened presents. Holly got new books from everyone. Pearl rolled her eyes at Holly's joke gift of the short story *To Build a Fire* but absolutely loved her new red panda plushie.

Holly and Bella had both chipped in to get Damien brand new D&D figures and they all promised to play soon.

Pearl gave everyone drawings of themselves as animals: Holly was a wolf, Damien a fox, Bella a flamingo, Rebel was a racoon, and Nicolas was a sparrow.

Nicolas got everyone gift cards to their favorite stores. Holly got Barnes and Noble, Damien got *The Orc Lair*, their local comic book and game shop, Rebel got Target, Bella got Nails R Us, and Pearl got REI.

Rebel had gotten them all candy so they couldn't bring it, but they all thanked Rebel anyway. Damien had forgotten to get presents for anyone except Holly so everyone else got IOUs.

When they were finally kicked out by the hospital staff Pearl skipped on her way to the car and said:

"Best Christmas ever!"

Holly smiled and said, "Best Christmas ever!"

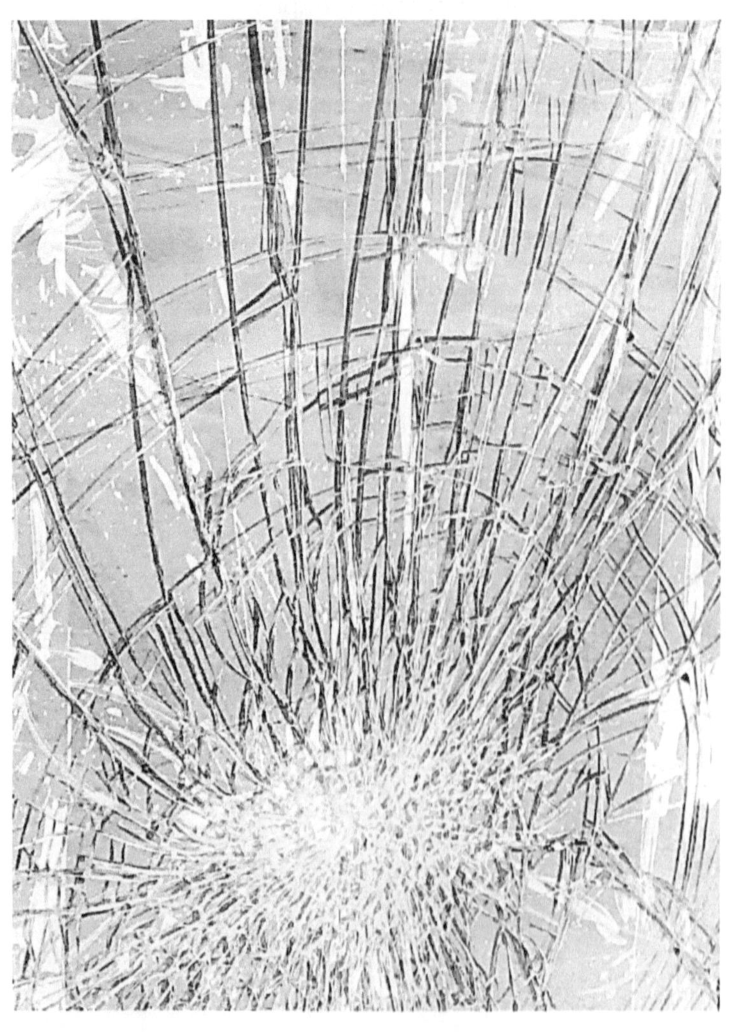

"For of all sad words of tongue or pen,
  The saddest are these: 'It might have been!' "

– John Greenleaf Whittier

MICHAEL GREEN WAS EIGHTEEN years old when he died. He was drunk out of his mind and in so much pain he could barely breathe. He was crying when he said goodbye to his little sister through a broken window with sirens screaming.

But he wasn't crying from the pain. He was crying because he loved his sister and was barely remembering that this wasn't the first time she had been his sister. Whispers of ancient Greek were at the back of his mind, memories of soft summers he had never lived in this life.

But in the end Michael Green's mind was kind. It let him be in so much shock in the end that the pain was almost gone. Michael's last memory of his most recent life was of his sister, kneeling in broken glass and twisted metal, his own bloody hand in hers, tears streaming down her face in the freezing cold. He noticed she didn't have any jacket on before his eyes drooped shut and death welcomed him like an old friend.

Michael Green died that Sunday at 2:37 in the morning. His sister

Holly had to be dragged away screaming by two policemen.

Of course, how Holly had come to be there was another story altogether.

She had not been fast asleep in her bed as her parents had thought. She was up that late because she was reading *As I Lay Dying* for a project at school. She hadn't read it before because she was reading what she considered to be far more interesting books and playing far more interesting games.

Then a text had come in from Holly's friend, who was always out late partying, that there had been an accident. A really, *really* bad accident. Holly didn't even wake her parents. She just pulled on sneakers and ran.

It was barely March and the nights were still cold but Holly ran anyway, seeing her breath in front of her face. When they were younger, she and Michael had pretended that they were dragons and the vapor from their mouths could level cities.

"It's going to be okay," she panted, "he crashed by the fire station, they'll save him. It's going to be okay."

It only took her five minutes to run to the fire station since it was so close by. That fact had been especially useful when she and Michael had tried to make cookies as a surprise for their parents and managed to set the oven—and half the kitchen—on fire.

She thought that maybe the car had burst into flames but pushed the thought from her mind and just let her adrenaline pump.

She heard the sirens before she saw what used to be Michael's car. There were police cars, yellow tape, an ambulance that wasn't open, and EMTs who were nowhere near the car.

Holly was about to yell at them when she overheard one of them say that the car and Michael were in just the wrong position and they couldn't get him out. They couldn't even get a blood transfusion in.

Holly dove under the yellow tape hoping against logic that Michael was somehow unhurt, like those skydivers that fell thousands of feet and just had some bruises.

Michael's car had swerved for nothing in the middle of the empty road. He had headed straight for a pole, hit it at just the wrong angle and that sent him careening towards the firehouse where his car rolled upside down. He was still in his seat; his seatbelt was jammed and the airbag hadn't deployed.

"Michael!" Holly yelled; she didn't care if the police saw her now. The driver's door had been cut away, the twisted metal was nearby, and shattered glass was everywhere. She could barely see Michael's head in the flickering headlights.

Holly was aware that a policeman was coming up behind her, but his words were static in her ears because her brother was dying in a car and she hadn't quite accepted it yet. But it was sinking in faster than she wanted it to.

"I'm his sister." The policeman let her go. She said it more for herself than the policeman; she had to convince herself that this was real because it felt like a sick joke, like a dream that would fade to nothingness and they would both be back at home safe and unhurt.

"H-Holly?" Michael rasped, there was blood rushing to his head and it did nothing to help his head wounds. Holly rushed forward and knelt in the broken glass, forcing herself to look at what used to be Michael's face.

"I'm here," she whispered, "I'm here."

"Holly? I think I fucked up." Michael sounded impossibly young; Holly wanted to cry because she realized in that moment that all the doctors in the world couldn't save him.

She couldn't save him.

"Yeah Michael," she said almost in tears, "I think you did."

"You—you need to find a picture of me," he slurred. He was still very drunk and Holly was so angry then, that she couldn't even say goodbye to her brother when he was in his right mind. "One you like. I want that to be how you remember me. Not like this."

In the back of Holly's mind, she realized that this was probably what amounted to Michael's suicide note.

"I-I didn't want to die like this," Michael said. Tears were already falling down his face the wrong way. "I wanted it to be quick, I d-didn't think I'd clip the pole."

"I don't want you to die," Holly said, even though she knew it was too late. Michael's mind had been made up when he went out that night and fate seemed determined to carry it through.

Michael's eyes were filling with tears and blood when he reached out the arm he could still feel. "Holly?" Holly's heart shattered. Michael sounded so hurt, so broken, so incredibly lost.

Holly crawled closer to the car and her brother and grabbed Michael's hand and tried not to look at the blood.

She took her hand and mechanically cleared the blood from his eyes. The car groaned like it would tip over further, would send Michael's head into the steering wheel for a second time.

Holly stayed. Michael's face cleared a bit, his tears no longer falling, but Holly began to cry instead. Holly tried to think of anything to say at all, a goodbye, a reassurance, but nothing wonderful came. No brilliant last words, no message to haunt her just, "I'm here, Michael. I'm not going to leave you."

"I know. That's why you're a better person than I am. I think you always have been."

There were a few ticks of silence then, "I'm gay."

"I know. Find a nice girl. Like Winona Ryder."

"She's a bit old for me."

"True…" Michael's eyes drooped shut for a second before they snapped back open, full of fear this time. "I don't think I want to die Holly. I-I want to see you grow up, and fall in love, and go to college, I want to be at your wedding and tell your wife about the time you knocked your own front teeth out with a rock by mistake. I want to live!"

"I know Michael." Holly rubbed his bloody knuckles and forced herself to meet his eyes, "I want you to live too."

"You—you gotta give my eulogy. Anyone else is just gonna fuck it up."

"I will. I promise." The world was crashing down around Holly too quickly, like she was sinking under water and no one would pull her up.

"You have to tell Mom I'm sorry—" He looked around wildly, "My God. Mom and Dad!"

"I'll tell them you're sorry. I'll tell everyone."

"I want Mom here," Michael said softly.

"Me too," Holly whispered. Their mother had always been strong and Holly desperately needed strength right now.

Then Michael started to laugh. Softly at first, then louder and louder and almost hysterically before he suddenly stopped.

"I'm going to die."

"Yes."

"And my God Holly it hurts so much."

"I know."

"This—this isn't your fault okay?" Michael's eyes were getting hazy. "It's mine. My fuckup. You're a good sister and a good person and—this isn't your fault."

"I know." Holly was aware she was crying but she made no move to clear her cheeks, she just held Michael's hand with both of hers. It did make her feel better that Michael said it, but she was so close to screaming.

Michael was crying again too, but he seemed much calmer. He looked much older. He looked her right in the eyes, smiled softly and said:

"Of all sad words of tongue or pen,

The saddest are these…"

And Michael Green died at 2:37 on a cold March morning.

Holly tried to force herself to finish it. Finish her brother's last words but she couldn't. His hand was limp and she was becoming aware for the first time that she was covered in his blood.

"Michael." No response. His eyes did not open, his chest did not rise. "MICHAEL!"

She tried to get closer to him but the car groaned once in warning and the policeman who had let the final exchange happen grabbed her and pulled her away. Michael's arm fell unresisting from her grip and she screamed.

She didn't stop screaming until the EMTs had put her in the back of the ambulance with a shock blanket on her shoulders. Her parents had been called and Holly's mind crashed down on her, replayed the scene over and over, what she should have said, should have done differently.

Then a rush of cold and exhaustion came over her and she fell into a dreamless sleep.

But right before sleep claimed her, she whispered, "It might have been!"

End of

We Few Old Souls

Book One

POETRY

AND

PROSE

AN ODE

TO

LANGSTON HUGHES

Nothing on this page can be true
I hardly know myself enough to tell it to you
I wear a million different masks, and a thousand smiles
And I take them with me on the roads, in the air for miles and
miles

What if I do not wish to know "you" or myself?
Is that why I run to the words, and the works, and the people on
the shelf?
"When shall we three meet again?
In thunder, lightning, or in rain?"
Do I simply live from verse to verse?

"Do I dare disturb the universe?"
What if I look and the person I find under all the masks is empty
and gaudy?
"Don't ever tell anybody anything. If you do, you start missing everybody."
What if there is indeed no rhyme or reason to the cruel, odd, and
challenging existence?
"He was soon borne away by the waves, and lost in darkness and distance."

I know a few scant things about myself and of my mind
Like scraps of paper they float by, amorphous and undefined
I know that I can talk about almost anything with complete ease
But talking about my true self makes me choke up and freeze
I know I am too morbid and macabre
Spending too much time reading about long slumbering evils and
el Chupacabra
I know that all too often I simply want to scream
And that reality is becoming more and more like a dream
I hope for things that cannot be
And let my daydreams wrap me in a world of fantasy

But to write a page about "you"
Well… who knows how much of this is really true?

The

Night

belongs

to

us

The cracked streets and dark alleys

The shining lights that blocked out stars, replacing them with buzzing streetlights

Are all for us

They beckon us forward, into the unknown

With shadow wrapped secrets and dark ideas

With buildings so familiar in the day, twisted to look like monsters and castles

All for us

Silent streets with roaring cars

Bridges lit up like Christmas trees

The skyline flickering like fire from the heat, bobbing like a mirage…

The night belongs to us

Freezing deserts with distant jagged peaks

A sky so packed with stars, you can see exactly where you could fall off the edge

Are all for us

The night is so much colder than the day

But we like it that way

All the coyotes and jackrabbits come out to play, away from the blazing sun and cracked earth

All for us

Cactuses silent and waiting

The moon large enough to swallow us all

With an owl singing in the distance, waiting for the sun to breach the clear sky…

The night belongs to us

The silent sea bobbing slowly,

A monster finally asleep and dreaming peacefully, letting its heartbeat tell stories in tides and the whispers of past storms

Are all for us

The soft moon is a respite from the cruel sun

The birds have long gone but the whales remain

The black sea reveals nothing, all vast secrets of history remain
softy covered carefully guarded

All for us

The sea will not turn over tonight

The sails flutter softly

Listening to the winds' soft melody drift across our ship,
lulling us into a deep calm slumber…

The night belongs to us

Fields rustling in the breeze

Storm clouds lazily rolling across the endless expanse of sky,
stars peek out between them

Are all for us

The day's humidity has stayed but not the ugly heat

For the sun has birthed fireflies

A million stars flickering up from the damp grass to join the
clouds and stars above

All for us

The roads silent but never dead

Creatures as wild as the wind skulk around

Bright eyes watch from the yard, watching and waiting and
longing for freedom

The Night **belongs** *to* us

THOUGHTS OF AN IDIOT AT A BUS STOP

USUALLY SOME RATIONAL PART of my mind would stop me from doing something this extraordinarily stupid, but that part of my brain must have been hungover because here I am.

At a bus stop at three in the morning with nothing besides a backpack and a terrible idea, waiting like an idiot.

I shouldn't even be here, I should be in bed quietly mourning my life falling to pieces. I should be convincing myself that Drew got what was coming to him, and at least he isn't my problem anymore.

But, as aforementioned, I'm at the goddam bus stop. At three in the fucking morning. Really not how I expected my summer before college to turn out. I just thought it would be like every other year: constant fighting and hiding in my room, just with the prospect of finally getting out when summer ended.

The hiding in my room used to be much more manageable since I actually used to *have* my own room. Then my dad decided that he was moving us across town to get away from "that conceited bitch" (our mother) and Drew and I were sharing a room.

Sharing a room with your almost-but-not-quite twin is bad enough, but then we were both fifteen and had raging hormones which led to many heated fights (the fact that we had no AC didn't help) that usually ended with one of us storming off and the other one apologizing later that day.

But Drew is my almost-but-not-quite twin and I am the older one and that means that I'm supposed to be the best. I'm supposed to protect him, from elementary bullies, from assholes on twitter, even from our parents.

From the police.

I'm supposed to stand up for him, fight for him, defuse a fight by asking our parents what happened that day, or bring up some celebrity feud, or turn the TV on to a stupid game show.

Except that doesn't work anymore, and I doubt Drew would go anywhere anyway. He's too proud to go to a center, but not everyone makes it. It's not my fault this happened, not even remotely.

I did everything I could to help him in school, tried to get him to stop smoking so much, I did everything I could have. I was on the other side of the world when he was kicked out.

Nothing I could have done.

My breath shows when I breathe out and shiver on the cold metal bench. It's so cold and so clear that I can actually see the stars. Drew and I used to count whatever stars we could see from the bus stops when we were younger, which is a memory so odd, so peaceful, that I'm shocked I thought of it.

I try to push it, find out where that flash of memory came from, but it slips like gossamer though the fingers of my mind and leaves me even colder and more confused when it goes.

It's two hours until the bus comes, and nothing is open around here this late. Drew and I used to go out late, run down the darkened streets and go to the Moon Market and buy ice cream and laugh all the way home.

Then the nights became longer and shorter and the ice cream became beer… It's better not to think about it. Or think about the fact that the old woman who ran the market knew I wasn't twenty-one but she gave the cans to me with a sad smile anyway.

I should be happy to be leaving that behind, but I'm 87% sure that happiness doesn't feel like a huge weight on your chest and mind.

I could still turn around. There is literally nothing stopping me. Because if I get on that bus I'm not going to look back. If I get on that bus, I'm going to be doing something stupid. I'll be at least forcefully checking him into rehab, or sneaking him into my dorm room. Probably both but in which order I don't know yet.

And I don't know if I want to.

Because I do better when he's not around. I don't have myself and someone else to look after. When my parents shipped him off to boarding school the summer of our junior year, I got the highest grades I ever got, when he slept at his friend's house I slept better, I didn't have to worry about him having a nightmare or running away.

It might be better for both of us if we never saw each other again.

But he's my brother. And he'd do the same for me, a thousand times over.

But this is stupid, for so many reasons. I should leave. I sigh as the headlights of the bus come into view, and my heart is heavy because I've made my decision.

I'm the only one on the bus.

NOM D. PLUME writes in a variety of genres…except for autobiography.

If you would care to write a review of TALES FROM AN ODD MIND in print or online, under your own name or a pseudonym, please do.

www.ingramcontent.com/pod-product-compliance
Lightning Source LLC
Chambersburg PA
CBHW031337060726
47590CB00007B/2509